THE WORLD'S ITCHIEST PANTS

Steve Hartley is a sensible man. He has a sensible job, a sensible family, lives in a sensible house and drives a sensible car. But underneath it all, he longs to be silly. There have been occasional forays into silliness: Steve has been a football mascot called Desmond Dragon, and has tasted World Record success himself – taking part in both a mass yodel and a mass yo-yo. But he wanted more, and so his alter ego – Danny Baker Record Breaker – was created. Steve lives in Lancashire with his wife and teenage daughter.

You can find out more about Steve
on his extremely silly website:
www.stevehartley.net

Books by Steve Hartley

DANNY BAKER RECORD BREAKER
The World's Biggest Bogey

DANNY BAKER RECORD BREAKER
The World's Awesomest Air-Barf

DANNY BAKER RECORD BREAKER
The World's Loudest Armpit Fart

DANNY BAKER RECORD BREAKER
The World's Stickiest Earwax

DANNY BAKER RECORD BREAKER
The World's Itchiest Pants

Look out for
DANNY BAKER RECORD BREAKER
The World's Windiest Baby

STEVE HARTLEY

DANNY BAKER RECORD BREAKER

THE WORLD'S ITCHIEST PANTS

ILLUSTRATED BY KATE PANKHURST

MACMILLAN CHILDREN'S BOOKS

First published 2011 by Macmillan Children's Books
a division of Macmillan Publishers Limited
20 New Wharf Road, London N1 9RR
Basingstoke and Oxford
Associated companies throughout the world
www.panmacmillan.com

ISBN 978-0-330-53329-4

Text copyright © Steve Hartley 2011
Illustrations copyright © Kate Pankhurst 2011

The right of Steve Hartley and Kate Pankhurst to be identified as the
author and illustrator of this work has been asserted by them in
accordance with the Copyright, Designs and Patents Act 1988.

1 3 5 7 9 8 6 4 2

A CIP catalogue record for this book is available from
the British Library.

Printed and bound in the UK by CPI Mackays Chatham ME5 8TD

For Rosie

This is entirely a work of fiction and any resemblance
to the real world is purely coincidental.

The Abominable
Snowboys

WARNING!

Look out!
There's a Squisher
about!

Drippy Noses

To the Keeper of the Records
The Great Big Book of World Records
London

Dear Mr Bibby

It's freezing here in Penleydale. Even the icicles have got icicles! The snow's taller than me in some places, and that means no school (Ace!), but also no football (Not Ace). My grandad knew it would happen. Three weeks ago a bee stung him on his knee and he came out with one of his sayings: 'When winter bees nobble your knees, there's bound to be a terrible freeze.' He reckons it'll last for ages.

← bee

Anyway, I've decided to make the most of it. Yesterday, I grew an icicle on the end of my nose. My best friend Matthew kept dribbling water down my conk and, as it froze, the icicle got longer and longer. It was 9.35 cm long before it fell off. I've sent a photo as proof. Is this the Longest Nose Icicle Ever?

me

icicle

Best wishes
Danny Baker

PS It's been a year since I broke my first record, and now I've got ten certificates on my bedroom wall, plus I helped my grandad win one too! Matthew's been keeping track of all my attempts and, as well as getting ten world records, I also tried to break thirty-one others. Who knows, one day I might break a world record for trying to break world records!

nose icicle!

The Great Big Book
of World Records
London

Dear Danny

I'm as excited as you are about all this snow,
because I'm looking forward to sending out lots
of certificates for new snow-based records in
the next few weeks. Hopefully one or two will
go to you! However, it won't be for the Nasal
Icicle-dangling record. Your dangle was a good
one, and just a drip or two short of the British
record, but well short of the world record.

The small, nomadic Mukpikluk tribe from the
North Pole wear traditional icicle jewellery
from their ears, nose, hair and fingers. In 1982,
to celebrate her hundredth birthday, the Chief
Tribal Elder Woman, Clotilda Littlefish, grew
a nasal icicle that was 128.55 cm long. It was
said that the beautiful tinkling music made by

5

her wonderful icicle body-ornamentation would
charm even the most ferocious of polar bears to
sleep, and so keep the tribe safe.

The world record for Mucus-enhanced Nasal
Icicle Dangling is held by Vladimir Popov,
of Tomsk in south-west Siberia. In the winter
of 1996, the temperature in the city fell to
a record low of -56 C. On the morning of
29 January Vladimir was waiting at his local
station for a train that was delayed due to
yaks on the line. He was suffering from a
heavy cold and had an extremely runny nose.
By the time his train arrived, five hours late,
Vladimir had a slimy green icicle that reached
from his nose to his feet, measuring 169.45 cm
in length. Amazingly, it had frozen solid to
the platform, and Vladimir was locked in place.
By the time firemen had cut him free, he had
missed the train.

'Popov's Pillar' of mucus is now kept in cold

storage during the short but warm Tomsk
summers. Every winter it is taken out and
placed on the platform, where it is used to
display notices about the late arrival of
trains and the dangers of not blowing your
nose.

Have lots of record-breaking fun in the snow,
Danny!

Best wishes
Eric Bibby
Keeper of the Records

Danny stood by the kitchen door pulling on his wellington boots as he and Matthew got ready to go out into the snow. Mum sat at the kitchen table, feeding baby Joey with warm milk from a bottle. He snuffled and gulped it down noisily.

'What have you two got planned for today?' asked Mum.

'We're going to check out the Sports Centre,' replied Danny. 'Jimmy Sedgley said that Ryan Biggs's sister's friend's auntie said the water in the pool is frozen solid. Jimmy said they're going to open it up for ice skating!'

'But the snow in town will be up to your belly-buttons!' exclaimed Mum.

'I've made us some snowshoes,' said Matthew, holding up one of four old tennis rackets with straps and buckles stuck to the frames. 'We just fix these to

the bottom of our
wellies, and our
weight gets
spread out so we
don't sink into
the snow.'

Just then,
Danny's big sister,
Natalie, shuffled into the kitchen to get her
breakfast.

'I feel terrible,' she grumbled, and blew a long
noisy *Hnnnnnnnnnnnnnk!* into a handkerchief.

Dad swallowed the mouthful of breakfast cereal
he was chewing, and sniffed. 'What's that smell?'
he asked.

Mum lifted Joey's bottom up to her face and
sniffed his nappy. She shook her head, then
glanced at Danny's feet. 'Are you trying to break
the world record for the stinkiest feet again?'

'No, I'm not!' protested Danny, sniffing the air
in the kitchen. 'Besides, when I tried to break *that*
record, my feet smelt a bit like boiled cabbage and

seaweed and eggs and cheese and drains all mixed together. This pong's *completely* different. It's more like cat pee . . .'

'And mouldy potatoes,' said Matt.

'And sour milk . . .' said Dad.

'And the elephant house at Walchester Zoo,' said Mum.

Danny followed his nose around the kitchen to find out where the smell was coming from, and it led him straight to his sister. 'It's Natalie Snotalie! *She's* the smell!'

'I am not!' she cried.

'You are!' said Mum, Dad and Matthew as they sniffed Natalie too.

'You've got Skunk Flu!' exclaimed Mum.

'Nooooooo!' wailed Natalie.

'They said on the news that it was spreading north,' said Dad. 'We'll have to let the doctor know and keep you indoors in case you give it to anyone else.'

'You have all the luck, Nats,' said Danny. 'I'd have to go without a bath for *months* to get as whiffy as you!'

As usual, Natalie made a grab to pull Danny's ears off. She stopped when something caught her eye through the kitchen window as Dad opened the curtains.

'Mum!' she whined. 'Tell him!'

Mum and Dad followed her gaze into the back garden and began to laugh. There was a snowman family sitting on the wooden bench beneath the white-topped branches of the cherry tree.

A big snow-Dad, with huge goalkeeper's gloves, sat in the centre of the group.

A smaller snow-Mum snuggled up to him, carrying a little snow-Joey.

On one end of the bench was a snow-Danny, wearing a Walchester United scarf and a naughty grin made of stones.

On the other end was a snow-Natalie, with

something long and green dangling from her red tomato nose.

'Who put those there, I wonder?' asked Dad, grinning at the boys.

Danny and Matthew shrugged and tried to look innocent.

Natalie blew her nose again. 'Mum! *Hnnnnnnnnnnnnnnk!* Tell them!'

'I'm telling you, boys,' said Mum, spraying the kitchen with rose-scented air freshener. 'There's nowhere near enough gunge coming out of that snow-Natalie's nose!'

Piggy Back

Dear Mr Bibby

Guess what? My sister Natalie's got
Skunk Flu! She's the first person in
Penleydale to catch it. Word soon
got round, and now everyone's been
told not to go out for the next two
weeks to stop it spreading.

atishoo!

Skunk flu

Nat had to go to the doctor today for tests,
but the snow was so deep around the house that
Dad couldn't get the car out. Then I had an
idea for a record attempt - Carrying a Sister
Piggyback Through the Snow! I carried her to
the doctor's using my snowshoes. Later
on, I carried her back home again.
Matt measured the distance and,
in total, I lugged her
for 5.62 Km.

me and Nat!

my snowshoes

Natalie sneezed all over me twenty-seven times on the way there and thirty-one times on the way back. I ended up covered in Skunk-flu snot-droplets, but I don't mind, because I want to catch it too! I've got a great plan. I'm going to offer to do jobs for her while she's ill and smelly, and stick as close to her as I can for as long as I can. Matthew says that'll be worse than having the flu! I don't care - Nat might be the first to have it, but I bet I'll be the stinkiest!

Did I carry my sister for a record-breaking distance? If not, I'll take her the long way round past the gasworks next time.

Best wishes
Danny Baker

ARE YOU A RECORD
BREAKER ?

Dear Danny

It was a great attempt at Snowbound-sister
Carrying (Piggyback), but you'll have to
go on a very big detour to the doctors if
you are going to beat the current record of
53.67 km, held by Ferris Rose of Jerry's Nose,
Newfoundland, Canada. His sister Doris didn't
know she was taking part in a record attempt
either. She thought Ferris was taking her to the
greengrocer's to buy a turnip. She reportedly
spent the last 10 km of the carry beating her
brother over the head with her wooden leg.

I should warn you that it is extremely
difficult to catch Skunk Flu, but if you do, the
symptoms can be nasty. There are three distinct
phases to the illness:

Phase 1: Explosive Sneezing and Pungent Body Odour (smelly sweat)

Phase 2: Sonorous and Malodorous Belching (loud and smelly burps)

Phase 3: Continuous Jaw Motion and Excessive Saliva Production (uncontrollable chinwagging and dribbling)

Although there are world records to be broken for each Skunk Flu Phase, if I were you I'd wear a mask and stay well away from your sister!

Best wishes
Eric Bibby
Keeper of the Records

Danny and Matthew spent all morning making snowmen in the deserted school playground. They had raided the school's overflowing big green wheelie bins and found an assortment of grubby items to add to their sculptures. They stood back to admire their work:

A model of their headteacher, Mr 'Beaky' Rogers, waited by the school gates, a bright orange traffic-cone nose sticking out from his face, below two black, soggy-tea-bag eyes. Nearby, at the crossing outside school, Mr Flutey the lollipop man had been built, his snowy arm outstretched, holding a half-chewed tutti-frutti-flavoured lollipop in his hand.

A sculpture of their teacher Mrs Woodcock filled the main entrance. Straggly, slimy spaghetti hair dangled from her enormous head, which was far too big to pass through the doors. Just around the corner, a snowy version of dinner lady Mrs

Gommersall stood in the kitchen doorway, wearing a greasy-paper-bag chef's hat and cooking up a battered old football boot in a rusty frying pan.

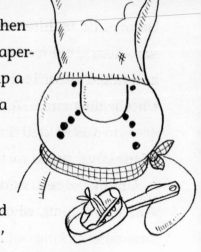

'They're better than the real thing!' laughed Danny.

'Someone's coming!' hissed Matthew. 'It's Creepy Cripps!'

The boys scurried behind the wheelie bins. Scrunching footsteps came towards them and then stopped. They heard Mr Cripps's familiar rasping cough as the caretaker studied the snowman of 'Beaky' Rogers. 'Someone'll be in trouble over this,' he wheezed.

Danny and Matthew waited quietly until Creepy Cripps had gone on his rounds, then they made a dash for the gates.

'That was close,' said Danny. 'We'd get detention for a squigga-squillion years if he'd caught us!'

The streets of Penleydale were empty. People had heeded the Skunk Flu Alert and were staying indoors. Great drifts of snow piled up against houses, smothering the roads and gardens. Huge flakes continued to swirl from the grey sky, adding to the thick white mantle. A strange, soft silence had settled over the valley, and the only sound was the scrunch of the boys' tennis rackets plunging into the snow.

Danny paused, staring along the deserted road. 'You know, Matt, what this town needs is people – snowpeople.'

Matthew glanced around to see if there was anyone looking. 'The coast's clear,' he replied. 'Let's get digging.'

Soon, snow-priest Father Paddy O'Hare sat on the low wall outside St Joseph's Church, sharing a comic with snow-Reverend Dave Goodie, vicar of St Waldebert-in-the-Bottoms.

'Hairy O'Hare isn't hairy enough,' said Danny, sticking short twigs in the snowman's ears and up his nose.

'And we forgot Mr Goodie's buck-teeth,' said Matthew, giving the Reverend a goofy grin made of orange peel.

Danny and Matthew continued through town, leaving a trail of funny footprints in the smooth, untouched snow. All the shops were closed, and the High Street looked like a still, white river winding between them.

Danny created a pair of feet sticking out of the mouth of the postbox on the corner, as though someone had fallen head-first into it.

At the bus stop, they built a snowy Snow White and seven snow-Dwarfs queuing patiently, while across the road a giant snow-rabbit was escaping from the greengrocer's shop carrying a huge snow-carrot. Danny dropped a small pile of round black pebbles under the animal's bottom.

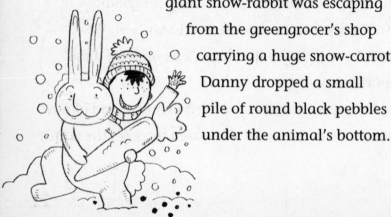

'It's what bunnies do,' he said, grinning at Matthew.

They were just adding the finishing touches to a model of a monster mouse chasing Pardon, the ferocious one-eared cat that lived in Gertie's Gum and Gobstopper sweet shop, when they heard the tinkle of a bell as the shop door opened.

The boys dived for cover in the doorway of the fish and chip shop nearby.

They heard the voice of Gertie Gubbins. 'When I find out who's poking fun at my Pardon,' she stormed, 'they'll be banned from my shop for good!'

'We need to be careful,' said Matthew. 'We'll cop for it if people find out it's us making these snowmen.'

'We need disguises,' replied Danny. 'And I know where I can get some.' He gazed through the empty chip-shop window, and his tummy gurgled. 'Let's go home for tea. Call for me super-early tomorrow. I've got a plan!'

As Danny opened the front door of his house, the pungent pong of Skunk Flu Stink slammed into his face. Dad stomped down the stairs wearing a white mask over his face, spraying the hall with 'Fiery Jock' his super-smelly footballers' muscle-rub.

'The air freshener's not covering up Natalie's pong,' he explained. 'I didn't think anything could smell worse than your feet Danny, but Natalie's managed it!'

The Abominable Snowboys

Overnight, there had been another heavy snowfall.
Super-early the next morning, Matthew called at
Danny's house.

'I raided Mum's jumble-sale bags last night,' said
Danny as the boys crept up to his bedroom. 'Look
what I've made.'

He opened the wardrobe door and showed
Matthew a costume made up of Dad's old cricket
jumper and a pair of Mum's stretchy white
leggings.

'This one's yours,' he said. 'And here's mine.'

Danny held up another outfit. The upper half
was one of Natalie's white disco tops. It was covered
in shiny circular sequins that glittered and sparkled
like tiny slivers of ice. He had added a pair of Dad's
white track pants, with the legs rolled up.

There were also threadbare white towels for

capes, white bobble hats with eyeholes cut out for masks, and two pairs of silver gloves.

'My Grandma Florrie's bedsocks will cover up our wellies,' said Danny as the boys put on their costumes over their ordinary clothes.

'Just one more thing.' He handed Matthew a pair of Dad's baggy old off-white Y-fronts. 'The best

superheroes wear their underpants on the *outside*.'

They gazed at themselves in the mirror.

'Ace!' said Danny.

'Cool,' agreed Matt.

Danny swirled his tatty bath towel across his body. 'With our Cloaks of Invisibility, no one will see us against the snow!'

'Let's go and make snowmen!' laughed Matthew, pretending to fly towards the bedroom door.

'Ace! I'll have to be back before lunch though,'

said Danny. 'I told Natalie I'd tidy her room and do her nails. It's all part of my plan to catch Skunk Flu from her.'

'I'll give you a hand,' said Matthew. 'I'll do the tidying, you do the nails!'

After a morning spent building more naughty snowmen, the boys sneaked back home. Danny hid their disguises at the back of his wardrobe and gave Matthew a paper flu mask before they entered Natalie's toxic room.

Matthew arranged Natalie's CDs in alphabetical order and sorted all her shoes into pairs, while Danny carefully painted his sister's fingernails with shiny pink varnish.

She sneezed. 'A . . . a . . . *atishooooo!'*

Danny felt the little droplets of sneeze-juice shower his face. Ace! he thought, breathing deeply and

filling his lungs with Natalie's germs.

'You've missed a bit,' she sniffed, snatching a handkerchief from a box with her free hand, and blowing her nose. '*Hnnnnnnnnnnnnnk!*'

Danny was just finishing the last fingernail when he heard a gurgling, burbling, slurping sound, like bath water being forced down a blocked drain. He looked up at Natalie. Her eyes were stretched wide in surprise and alarm, and her cheeks ballooned out as though she was blowing an invisible trumpet. Then her mouth gaped like a goldfish and she let out a window-rattling, ear-splitting, hair-raising, rotten-egg-whiffing burp, right in Danny's face.

'Mega Ace!' he cried.

'Mega Cool!' agreed Matthew.

'You've got Skunk Flu Phase Two!' Danny told his sister. 'How's your chin?'

'Why?' replied Natalie, frowning with worry.

'Because I can't wait to see Phase Three!'

Just then, Mum came into the bedroom, also wearing a mask. In one hand she held a copy of the *Penleydale Clarion*, and in the other, one of

baby Joey's
particularly
dirty, gooey
nappies,
which she waved
in front of her.

'I know this smells
disgusting, but it's a lot better than Natalie!'

She glanced out of the bedroom window and
smiled. 'There's one of those silly snow-sculptures
that have been appearing all over town!'

A small snow-kennel nestled in the far corner
of next door's garden. A perfect copy of Buster,
their bull-terrier dog, stood with his leg cocked up
against a rhododendron bush nearby, as if frozen in
place by the Arctic weather.

'It's front-page news,' said Mum. 'Look, I've
brought the paper to show you.'

Danny and Matthew gazed at a photograph
of the vampire they had built emerging from a
wheelie bin outside Gracie Green's house. Danny
grinned as he read the short article:

THE PENLEYDALE CLARION

SNOWMEN INVADE PENLEYDALE!

By Reginald Heap, Chief News Reporter

Dozens of cheeky snowmen and funny snow-animals are springing up all over town, and no one knows who's making them.

'It's fantastic!' said Sticky Bun delivery man Dave Duck, aged 23, who found a snowman riding his motorbike.

'It's disgraceful!' said teacher Mrs Woodcock, age unknown, when told of the snowy version of her outside Coalclough Primary School. 'I'd like to get my hands on

the culprit.'

'It's a mystery,' said Police Sergeant Percival Plodder, aged 45. 'Our only clue is the strange footprints around each one, like a huge flat-footed one-toed monster – perhaps it's the Abominable Snowman!'

'I wonder who's making them?' said Mum.

Just then, Natalie's chin started to waggle up and down like a monkey chewing a mint. Long, sticky strands of drool dribbled and dangled from her lips.

'That's Skunk Flu Phase Three!' laughed Danny. 'You'll have to wear a bib like baby Joey!'

'Mum!' wailed his sister. Her chin wagged furiously, sending ropes of spit flying in all directions. 'Tell him!'

Squished!

Dear Mr Bibby

Look at the newspaper clipping I've sent with this letter. I know you'll keep our secret, so I can tell you. It's not the Abominable Snow*man* making these snowmen, it's the Abominable Snow*boys* – me and Matt! We've made special suits to hide our identities and built an igloo HQ in the corner of my front garden. It's Ace!

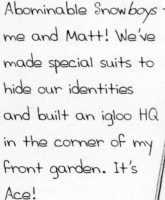

we made these! ↗

No one's caught us yet, and so

far we've made forty-nine snowy sculptures!
Matt's taking a photo of each one as proof.

What's the record for building the most
snowmen in a single town?

Best wishes
Danny Baker

ARE YOU A RECORD
BREAKER?

Dear Danny

If the Big Freeze lasts for as long as the
weather forecasters say it will, you and
Matthew should certainly have enough time to
break the Single-location Team-snowman-building
world record! However, you're going to have to
work hard.

In 1988, Merrick Moth of Newbiggin-by-the-Sea,
formed 'The Snowdrops', a group of friends who
loved all things chilly. In November that year,
the group made 445 individual snowmen in the
Norwegian town of Lillehammer. Their creations
were nothing like the wonderful sculptures you
and Matthew have produced in Penleydale, but
they broke the record.

In 1991, The Snowdrops fell out over which flavour of ice-lolly was best. The group split up, and Merrick Moth set off alone to tackle the record for High-altitude Single-handed Snowman Building. He built a snowman on top of the ten highest mountains in the world, finishing his amazing feat by constructing one on the peak of Mount Everest.

However, when Merrick stuck the carrot in the snowman's face to make the nose, he pushed too hard and the head fell off. It rolled down the long steep slopes gathering speed and snow, getting bigger and bigger by the second. It bowled into Base Camp at the same time as Sherpa Ninezing, who had just discovered the lair of the legendary Yeti, otherwise known as the 'Abominable Snowman'. Sadly, the humongous snowball rolled over poor Sherpa Ninezing, flattening him like a pancake before he could reveal the location to anyone else.

Although Merrick Moth never intended to break this record, the snowball he started when he accidentally knocked his snowman's head off was the biggest ever recorded, with a circumference of 103.68 m. Because of the cold and high altitude in the Himalayas, the snowball will never melt and remains at Base Camp for all time as a unique memorial to poor Sherpa Ninezing.

Good luck with your attempt, Danny, and don't worry – your snowy secret's safe with me!

Best wishes
Eric Bibby
Keeper of the Records

'How's Nat the Niff?' asked Matthew as one of Natalie's booming belches burst from her room next door.

'Still stinky,' replied Danny. 'Dad's hung strings of garlic around her bedroom and left lumps of runny green cheese all over the house to try and cover the whiff. But it doesn't work now she's letting rip with those 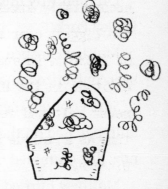 mega-pongy burps as well. *And* her chin's started wagging like a jelly on a spring. She's not happy!'

Just then, Dad came upstairs and popped his head round Danny's bedroom door.

'There's been a terrible accident on the High Street,' he announced. 'Snow White and the Seven Dwarfs have been run over at the bus stop – they're splattered!'

'What?' said Danny.

'It's true,' continued Dad. 'And the snow-bunny outside the greengrocer's has had his ears cut off and his carrot pinched!'

The boys stared at each other.

'Let's go and investigate!' said Danny.

On their way into town, the boys passed through Penley Park.

Matthew gasped. 'Look!' he cried. 'Our parrot's been pulverized and our budgie's been battered!'

Sure enough, the two huge snow-birds they had built perched on the swings in the playground were now just crumpled heaps of snow.

Matthew hurried over to check the crocodile they had made hiding by the DANGER! sign on the railings around the pond. 'The crocodile's been crunched!'

Danny clomped over to

the see-saw, where they had left a snow-hamster and a snow-hippo riding happily. 'Our hamster's been hammered!' he said. 'And what's this?'

In the pile of snow
that used to be the
hippo was a small
rectangular card.
It was impaled there with
an icicle, and on it was written in black, spidery
handwriting:

'STOP THIS NOW OR THE DUCKS GET IT!'

They tramped over to the bandstand, where
Matthew had built a mother duck being followed
by a row of ten tiny baby ducks.

'My ducklings have been destroyed!' he groaned,
picking up a second notice, covered in the same
squiggly writing. The sign had been jabbed into one
of the trampled sculptures:

'THE DUCKS GOT IT ANYWAY!'

Just then, Danny noticed two straight lines
cutting through the snow, going from one bashed

snow-model to another.

'Look!' he said, pointing at the marks. 'Ski tracks! And they're heading into town! Let's check out the High Street.'

It was just as Dad had described. A small crowd had gathered to look at the flattened remains of Snow White and the Seven Dwarfs. Another message had been scratched into the ice covering the window of Bewley's Bakery:

'DON'T BE DOPEY!
YOU'RE MAKING ME GRUMPY!'

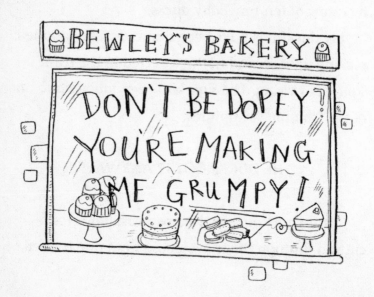

'Our snowmen have been squished,' said Matthew. 'What'll we do?'

'We'll rebuild them all tomorrow!' whispered Danny. 'This is a job for the Abominable Snowboys!'

Snow Wars

Matt called for Danny straight after breakfast the following day.

'I've hidden our disguises in the HQ,' said Danny. 'Let's go!'

The boys scurried down to the corner of the front garden, crawled into the igloo and put on their disguises. They grinned at each other, pulled down the bobble-hat masks and put their underpants on over their overpants.

'The Abominable Snowboys are go!' said Danny, peeking out of the entrance to make sure Natalie wasn't watching from the house. 'All clear!'

He and Matthew scuttled across the snow and headed down the road to

check on the snowmen they had built at school.

'The Squisher's been busy again,' said Danny as they approached the gates.

Mr Flutey's arm had been broken off, and the tutti-frutti lolly shoved up his nose. 'Beaky' Rogers was just a shapeless white mound with the orange cone on top, and the snowy dinner lady, Mrs Gommersall, had been chopped and sliced like a loaf of bread. Mrs Woodcock's huge head had been knocked off and yet another note skewered to it with a long glistening icicle:

'DON'T LOSE *YOUR* HEADS!!! YOU HAVE
BEEN WARNED!!!'

The boys made quick repairs to Mrs Gommersall and Mr Flutey, then heaved Mrs Woodcock's head back on to her body.

'It's back to front,' said Matthew.

'It doesn't matter,' replied Danny. 'She looks better that way.'

He scribbled a defiant message of his own on

the back of the note and stabbed it into the snow-teacher's back:

'WE'LL STAY ONE STEP A-HEAD OF YOU!'

Danny and Matthew
made their way into town.
This time there was no
need to duck into doorways
or creep around corners
– their disguises hid their
identities – and they were
able to take their time
repairing all the spoilt snowmen.

Whenever the boys came to a nasty notice, they
flipped the card over and wrote a cheeky reply:

'WE'RE NOT SNOWFLAKES!'

And:

'WE WON'T MELT AWAY!'

And:

'YOU'VE GOT SNOW BUSINESS WRECKING
OUR SNOWMAN!'

And:

'WE ARE THE ABOMINABLE
SNOWBOYS!'

Outside the Woof and Fluff Animal Hospital,
Danny and Matthew decided to make some brand-
new snow-sculptures. They dug and shaped,
making a queue of animals waiting for the vet to
arrive.

At the front stood the
Big Bad Wolf being
chased by the Three Little
Pigs; next in line came
Nellie the Elephant being
frightened by the Three
Blind Mice, and bringing

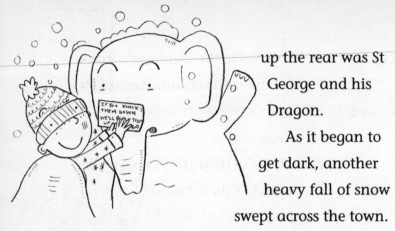

up the rear was St
George and his
Dragon.

As it began to
get dark, another
heavy fall of snow
swept across the town.

A small crowd of people who had stopped to watch
the boys clapped and cheered as Danny stuck a
final message on the end of Nellie the Elephant's
trunk:

'IF YOU KNOCK THEM DOWN, WE'LL BUILD
THEM UP AGAIN!'

'Time to go home,' he said. 'We'll see what
happens tomorrow.'

The next morning, the boys followed a fresh
trail of ski tracks through the town. Every single
snowman they had made or repaired had been
smashed to the ground during the night.

'Look at this,' said Matthew, pointing to the note

Danny had left on Nellie the Elephant's trunk.

On the back of the card was another spidery scrawl:

'IF YOU BUILD THEM UP, I'LL KNOCK
THEM DOWN AGAIN!'

'It said on TV that the Big Thaw will start in three days,' said Matthew. 'If the Squisher keeps squishing, we'll just run out of time.'

Danny thought for a moment. 'We *can* still break the record,' he said, setting off for home. 'I've got a letter to write, and this time it's not to Mr Bibby!'

Great Galloping Snowballs!

To the Editor
The Penleydale Clarion
Wapping Street

Dear Sir

Please can you print this notice on your front page:

Calling all kids!
The Abominable Snowboys need your help!

SNOWBOYS
NEED YOU!

We've been trying to break the world record
for single-location Team-snowman Building, but
there's a sinister Squisher spoiling our attempt.

Come to Penley Park at 9 o'clock on Saturday
morning. If we all work together, we can
break the record and squash the Squisher
before the Big Thaw starts!

Best wishes
The Abominable Snowboys

PS Don't forget to bring a spade and a packed
lunch!

On Saturday morning, Danny and Matthew went into their igloo HQ and put on their superhero outfits for the last time. The suits were already looking the worse for wear, floppy and grubby, the overpants-underpants baggier than ever and only held up by safety pins. They strapped on their snowshoes and made their way to Penley Park.

Dozens of children had already turned up, each one armed with a spade and kitted out in woolly hats, scarves and mittens. The kids cheered when they saw the Abominable Snowboys galumphing towards them.

'Cool!' said Matthew. 'It's an Abominable Army!'

'Come on everyone!' shouted Danny. 'Let's make a game of snowman football!'

More helpers turned up throughout the morning. By the time they all stopped to eat their packed lunches, two teams of snowy footballers dotted the pitch, with a snow-referee in the centre, and two assistant referees on each touchline. One player had been made rolling around with a fake injury. Another was frozen in place making a desperate sliding tackle on his opponent, who had just taken a shot at goal. The snow-goalkeeper ('That's me!' said Danny) was diving across his goal line to save the shot. The snowman crowd around the edge was growing rapidly, and Matthew struggled to keep a count of them all.

By four o'clock in the afternoon, with the light beginning to fade, Matthew announced that they had made 441 snowmen.

'We've got more spectators here than Penleydale United!' said Danny. 'Only five more to build and we're record breakers!'

The kids cheered once more.

Just then, Danny heard a distant rumble, like thunder. He glanced up towards the darkening sky and an astonishing sight met his eyes.

Careering down the steep hill behind the park at a terrifying speed was the most enormous snowball Danny had ever seen. With every passing metre, it collected more and more snow, growing bigger and bigger, travelling faster and faster.

'It's heading straight towards us!' gasped Danny.

The Abominable Army stopped, staring in awe as the snowball hurtled along the edge of town.

'Oh no!' shouted Matthew, pointing frantically in the opposite direction. 'Look!'

A second giant snowball was thundering down the other side of the valley. It had been

carefully aimed and nothing stood in its way. In seconds it would roll right into the park, flattening snowmen and children alike.

'RUN!' yelled Danny. 'Get out of the way!'

Everyone scattered in panic. The two converging monster snowballs –
each one as big
as a house –
crashed into
the park at
the same
moment. One
smashed over
the Happy
Cuppa Tea
Rooms, while the
other reduced the wooden

bandstand to splinters. They steamrollered through the multitude of snowmen, before crunching to a halt a short distance from each other in the middle of the snow football pitch. Only the snow-goalkeepers at each end had escaped the crush.

As shocked children stood and stared, an eerie silence settled, broken only by a weird muffled buzzing coming from the snowballs, as though each was filled with a million angry bees.

'The Squisher's beaten us after all,' said Matthew.

Danny gazed at the devastation and had to admit that Matthew was right: the record attempt lay in ruins. Just then, movement in the trees nearby caught Danny's eye. A hooded figure was zigzagging through the trees on long black skis.

'It's him! It's the Squisher!' said Danny, scooping up a big snowball and hurling it at the moving target. His aim was spot-on: right on the nose! The snowball splattered across the man's face, and he tumbled to the ground.

'Don't let him get away!' ordered Danny.

The Abominable Army swarmed into the woods.

They surrounded the mysterious raider, pelting him with dozens of snowballs, turning him instantly into a living snowman.

Danny and Matthew worked their way to the front of the crowd of children. 'Why have you been spoiling our fun?' asked Danny.

The man struggled to his feet, tugged off his  hood and fixed the boys with black, beady eyes. He had a long, bony face framed by wispy grey hair that stuck out untidily in all directions.

'My name is Merrick Moth,' he announced. 'My Snowdrops and I have held this record since 1988, and I'm not about to let a couple of kids take it away. I warned you, but you wouldn't stop.' He glanced around at the destruction he had caused. 'I win! You lose!'

Matthew stepped forward. 'You could have squashed us all with those giant snowballs!' he said.

'Let's tie him up with our scarves,' said Danny. 'Then take him to the police station!'

The Abominable Army swarmed around the Squisher to stop him from escaping, then knotted their scarves together, wrapping the thick woolly rope tightly around him.

'Wait!' he called as the throng of children slid him on his skis towards the park gates. He stared at Danny and Matthew. 'Who are *you*?'

'We're the Abominable Snowboys!' they replied in chorus.

'Also known as . . .' said Danny, as he and Matthew yanked the bobble hats off their heads,

'Danny Baker.'

'And Matthew Mason!'

The rest of the kids burst out laughing. 'We

knew it was you as soon as we heard you wanted to break a world record!'

Danny and Matthew grinned at each other and watched as the jostling crowd of children headed for the police station with the tall figure of Merrick Moth trapped at its centre.

Alone again in the park, the boys took one last look around the field of flattened footballers.

'What's this?' said Danny, digging a small black box from the snow. The device had a long silver aerial and two joysticks with the words 'Left Ball' and 'Right Ball' written beneath them.

'Remote-controlled snowballs!' gasped Matthew. 'Cool!'

'So *that's* why they're buzzing,' said Danny, staring at the two huge spheres. 'I wonder . . .'

He touched the left joystick, and one of the snowballs jerked forward. He moved the right joystick, and the other snowball began to creep across the ground.

'If we're quick, Matt, we might *still* be able to claim a record.'

Danny Baker Record Breaker

Dear Mr Bibby

You need to send Merrick Moth another certificate, for Remote-controlled Giant-rolling-snowball Snowman Destruction! But you'd better send it to Bad Bodkin Prison, because that's where he'll be living for the next six months! He's been charged with rolling snowballs with intent to cause grievous bodily harm!

Prison!!

He squished our record attempt with his two great big snowballs, but we had the last laugh – me and Matt managed to turn them into a great big snow-bum! It measures 111.36 m all the

snow-bum!

ACE

way round. It's huge and it's awesome, but is it a record breaker?

Best wishes
Danny Baker

PS Even though the Big Thaw started today, my dad says that our snow-bottom is so massive it won't melt for weeks! Ace!

Dear Danny

I read all about Merrick Moth's terrible
deeds, and he is now banned from future record
attempts. I will NOT be sending him any more
certificates ever again. However, his disgraceful
behaviour has led to yet another stunning
achievement by you and Matthew!

That snow-bottom is one of the most truly
wonderful creations I have ever seen! I have
framed the photograph you sent, and it now
hangs in my office where everyone can see it.

Congratulations! You and Matthew have set a new
world record for the Biggest Snow-bottom Ever
Made! You should be very proud! I have enclosed
another certificate to add to your collection.

Best wishes

Eric Bibby

Keeper of the Records

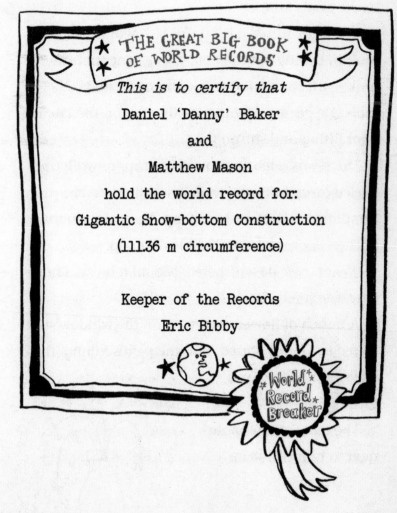

★ THE GREAT BIG BOOK ★
OF WORLD RECORDS

This is to certify that

Daniel 'Danny' Baker

and

Matthew Mason

hold the world record for:

Gigantic Snow-bottom Construction

(111.36 m circumference)

Keeper of the Records

Eric Bibby

World Record Breaker

The Big Freeze was over, and the Big Return to School was about to begin. Danny was up early and sat at the kitchen table sprinkling sugar on his bowl of cereal. He sniffed and wiped his nose on the sleeve of his jumper.

Just as he raised a spoonful of cereal to his mouth, Danny felt the floor move beneath his feet and heard something crack and creak under the table. He peered down to see the tiles on the kitchen floor lifting and shifting.

There was a tearing sound as strips of wallpaper peeled away from the walls around the room, tumbling to the floor in a heap. The paint on the kitchen door started to bubble and pop.

'What. . . ?' he whispered. 'Could it be . . . Phase One: the smelly sweat?'

A bunch of flowers in a vase on the window sill wilted as Danny stared at it, the petals falling, the leaves shrivelling and turning brown.

The toast on the plate next to him curled up

at the corners, and the milk in his bowl of cereal curdled into thick, cheesy lumps.

'And . . .' Danny's nose began to itch and twitch, 'the explosive sneezes?'

The tickling became more intense. Suddenly, a booming, thunderous sneeze exploded from him, peppering his breakfast bowl with bogeys, and splattering congealed milk and soggy cornflakes far and wide.

'A . . . A . . . A . . . TISHOOOOOOOOOOOOOO!'

Upstairs, he heard Dad cry out, 'We've got a gas leak!'

'It's not gas, it's ME!' shouted Danny, doing an excited jig around the kitchen. 'I've got it at last! I've got Skunk Flu!'

He heard the sound of feet rushing down the stairs, and a moment later Natalie burst into the room, followed by Mum and Dad.

'Phwoar!' sneered his sister. 'What a horrible . . .' She got no further. Her face turned green, her eyebrows shot up in surprise and she crumpled to the floor in a dead faint.

Mum gasped and
staggered backwards,
covering her face
with the collar of
her dressing gown,
her hair coiling into
ringlets in the toxic air.

Dad held his arm over his
mouth and nose and dashed for the kitchen door,
yanking it open just as Matthew arrived to pick
Danny up for school. The cloud of Skunk-flu Stink
surged out of the door, lifting Matthew off his feet
and dumping him on
his behind in the
melting snow.

'Awesome!'
he spluttered,
breathing in
the thick, sickly
odour. 'Your plan
worked! You smell
like . . . a blocked toilet

in a rotten-egg factory!'

'And a dead kipper down a drain,' added Mum.

'And an orang-utan's armpit,' added Dad.

Natalie added nothing: she was still unconscious on the floor.

'Runny green cheese and Joey's sloppy nappies aren't going to cover *this* pong,' continued Dad. 'We're going to need gas masks!'

'Ace!' grinned Danny. 'I'm *definitely* going to have the World's Whiffiest, Waggiest, Burpiest, Record-breakingest Skunk Flu Ever!'

Ants in
His Pants

WARNING!
This story will
make you
itch!

Silly-billy-dilly-dally-bing-bang-bong

To the Keeper of the Records
The Great Big Book of World Records
London

Annwyl Mr Bibby (That means 'Dear Mr Bibby' in Welsh)

We're having a Welsh Week at school, because my class is going to the Phwllwygol-y-wig Adventure Centre in North Wales (our teacher says it's pronounced Poo-wiggly-wig! Ace!). We've been singing in Welsh, baking slimy seaweed bread, wearing funny black hats, eating

me in a Welsh hat!

leek soup and playing rugby (it's not as good as football).

We've also made funny walking sticks called Tallypant Twytty-Knockers. They're shaped like a daffodil, and in the mountains around Poo-wiggly-wig they play a game called the Twytty-Knocker Grab. You drop a pile of the sticks on the ground, bounce a ball as high as you can, grab a few sticks and then catch the ball. You keep doing it until you drop the ball. The winner is the person who's collected the most twytty-knockers.

Twytty-Knockers

It's really hard, but I kept practising and managed to grab seventeen sticks! Is there any chance I've broken a record?

Best wishes
Danny Baker

PS I was hoping to get the chance to ride the scariest rollercoaster in the world, the Pontypyddl PantWetter, when I'm in Wales, but my dad says it's in a different part of the country. Not Ace!

The Great Big Book
of World Records
London

ARE YOU A RECORD
BREAKER?

Dear Danny

You will feel at home at the Phwllwygol-y-wig Adventure Centre: it's a record breaker! It has the biggest domed wigwam in Wales: 'The Wygol-y-wigwam'. It is 21 m high at the centre and has a circumference of 135 m.

The ancient game of Twytty-knocker Grabbing is only played in Phwllwygol-y-wig, because that is the only place where you find the Tallypant Twytty. This is a rare breed of Welsh mountain sheep, who has a right leg shorter than its left leg, so that it can walk straight across the steep mountain hillsides without falling over. However, it can only go in one direction, because as soon as it turns round, it *does* fall over. Local farmers use the twytty-knocker to drive the sheep backwards across the mountain so they can begin grazing again.

The world record for grabbing the sticks is seventy-three, by Champion Twytty-knocker Grabber Olwyn Humphries of Abersoch, so your attempt was an excellent one, but well short of the best.

Enjoy your stay in Wales, Danny.

Best wishes
Eric Bibby
Keeper of the Records

'Look at the size of that wigwam!' said Danny, peering through the window as the coach pulled to a halt in a forest clearing that was the Phwllwygol-y-wig Adventure Centre. 'Mr Bibby says it's a record breaker!'

Danny and Matthew stared out at a huge domed building in the centre of the clearing. It was made of brown canvas stretched over long, curving tree trunks, and seemed to have grown like a big pimple from the forest floor.

Two long, wide wooden huts stood on either side of the wigwam, one painted custard-yellow, the other gooseberry-green, while a row of ten conical tents signposted 'The Pee-pee Teepees' stood behind it. Towering trees with trunks as straight as pencils pressed in on the clearing, enclosing it like a fence. Clumps of daffodils burst from the ground for as far as Danny could see, like little glowing fountains of green and gold in the shadowy forest.

'Girls, follow me to the girls' cabin,' called Miss Dunderhead, stepping out of the coach and striding away to the yellow hut.

'Lads are in the green cabin,' said Mr 'Polly' Parrot. 'Find a bed and unpack your things. If anyone wants the toilet, you'll find them in the Pee-pee Teepees on the far side of the giant wigwam in the middle of the camp.'

Danny and Matthew grabbed their packs and raced across the muddy ground.

'Bunk beds!' exclaimed Danny as he pushed through the door at one end of the hut. 'Ace!'

'I bags the bottom bunk!' said Matthew, diving on to the nearest empty bed.

'I bags the top bunk!' laughed Danny, clambering up the wooden ladder two steps at a time and hanging upside down making monkey noises at his friend.

The ten other boys from Danny's class charged into the hut to claim their bunks. They were soon followed by around ten boys from another school, and playful pillow fights broke out.

'What school are you from?' asked one of the new kids, bashing Danny over the head with his pillow.

'Coalclough Primary,' replied Danny, laughing

and fighting back. 'What about you?'

'We're from . . .' But before the boy could answer, Mr 'Polly' Parrot yelled 'QUIET!' and the hut fell silent. 'Leave your bags on your beds and get over to the wigwam for the Welcome Powwow,' he ordered. 'Take your wellies off and leave them outside on the left of the entrance.'

The boys funnelled out of the hut and hurried across the clearing.

'Ace!' gasped Danny as they entered the wigwam.

'Cool!' agreed Matthew.

The curving canvas roof rose high above them like a massive cave. It was painted white and decorated all over with drawings of animals and trees. The floor was covered with colourful square rugs, and the space buzzed with the excited chatter of dozens of kids sitting cross-legged on them.

Teachers from the two schools directed the boys to one side of the wigwam and the girls to the other. Danny and Matthew found a space on a rug and sat down.

Suddenly, with a loud cry of 'Geronimo!', a man

and woman swung over the children's heads into
the wigwam on ropes, landing nimbly like cats
in front of the audience. The man
had curly blond hair and wore a
gooseberry-green sweatshirt. He
raised a short wooden whistle to
his lips and blew:

'QUAAAAAAAACK!
QUACK! QUACK!'

'G'day!' he yelled.
'Welcome to the Wygol-
y-wigwam, the biggest in
the world! What a ripper gang
of ankle-biters you are! My name's
Bradley Tucker, but you can call me "Bush"! I'm
from Australia and I'll be in charge of all these
Bonzer Boys!' He waved his arms, encouraging his
side of the room to cheer loudly.

The woman was dressed in a custard-yellow
fleece and had pulled her long black hair into a
flopping ponytail. 'My name's Bunny Grylls,' she
announced. 'I'm an Aussie too, and I'm Leader

of the Gobsmacking Girls!'

The girls' side of the room tried to out-cheer the boys. Bunny blew hard on an owl whistle to settle the kids down again: 'HOO-HOOOOOO! HOO-HOOOOOO!'

'We've got oodles of awesome adventures, crazy crafts and cool competitions for you this week,' Bunny continued. 'And it's boys versus girls all the way!'

'But first, the Camp Rules,' said Bush. 'Number One: every time you meet one of your mates, you must use the camp greeting, which is: Silly-billy-dilly-dally-bing-bang-bong!'

The kids began to laugh and chatter again, until a blast on Bush's duck whistle made them quiet once more.

'Rule Number Two,' said Bunny. 'You get up at six thirty when you hear the Wakey-wakey Hooter.'

She gave three blasts on a klaxon horn. 'And you go to sleep, Lights Out at nine thirty, straight after you hear the Curfew Kazoo,' she added, pulling an instrument from her pocket and tooting a silly tune.

'Rule Number Three,' said Bush. 'No one is allowed out of their hut after we blow the Curfew Kazoo. If you want to go to the toilet in the night, you'll need a Pee-pee Pass-out.'

'If you're caught outside after Lights Out without a Pass-out,' said Bunny, 'you'll have to do the Poo-wiggly-wig Wipe-up.'

'Llewellyn, the security guard, and his guard goose, Gwyneth, patrol the camp after dark,' continued Bush. 'And let me tell you, you don't want to meet gruesome guard-goose Gwyneth on a dark night in the forest. She's as cranky as a frog in a sock!'

Bunny nodded. 'Too right, Bush! The competitions start this arvo, right after lunch, with a woodland bottom-shuffle relay race.'

At that moment an excited yelp burst from the girls' side of the room.

'DANNY!'

All faces
turned to stare
at a girl waving
frantically in
Danny's direction.
She wore a crimson
jacket and her
bright red hair was twisted into two tight pigtails.

She pointed at Danny and squealed, 'That's my boyfriend!'

Danny's tummy did a somersault and his toes curled up inside his socks. He ducked down, his face burning, as all faces swivelled round to stare at *him*.

'I don't believe it,' he hissed at Matthew. 'It's Sally Butterworth!'

'We met in
Spain last
summer,'
Sally yelled
to everyone.
'And we've got

the world record for kissing in a tree!'

'Woooooooooooooooooooooo!' whistled the other kids, laughing with delight.

Danny looked for somewhere to hide, but he was stuck. Bunny blew hard on her owl whistle – HOO-HOOOOOO! HOO-HOOOOOO! – and the room fell silent once again.

'What a rip-snorter of an idea for a competition!' she laughed. 'Maybe tomorrow you two can show everyone how it's done!'

'No way!' shouted Danny, scrunching up his face. 'I'm allergic to girls. They give me spots.' He pulled his jumper over his head, trying desperately to disappear.

The powwow finished with Bush and Bunny teaching the kids the camp song and holding a competition to see who could sing it loudest:

'Always eat when you are hungry.

Always drink when you are dry.

Always wash when you are dirty.

Always smile and never cry.'

'The Gobsmacking Girls are first on the

scoreboard!' yelled Bunny. 'I say we definitely won that one!'

When it was over, Danny and Matthew tried to sneak from the wigwam, but Sally Butterworth was too quick and ambushed them by the entrance.

'Silly-billy-dilly-dally-bing-bang-bong,' chirped Sally, smiling at the boys. 'I didn't know *you'd* be here.'

'Silly-billy-dilly-dally-bing-bang-bong,' said Danny, trying to ignore the grins of the other boys as they pushed past.

There was a small dark-haired girl standing just behind Sally. 'This is my best friend, Vicky Wilmott,' she said. 'Vicky's *brilliant* at maths, just like you Matt. She can do really hard sums in her head.'

'143,967,552 multiplied by 3,718,' said Danny.

Vicky frowned, and stuck her tongue out the corner of her mouth while she worked out the answer.

'535,271,358,336,' she replied.

Matthew pulled a calculator out of his coat pocket, and tapped in the numbers. He gaped at Danny. '3.6 seconds, and she's right,' he said. 'Cool!'

'19,674,887 divided by 7,833,' said Danny.

Vicky screwed her face up once more. '2,511.79459.'

'Mega cool!' gasped Matthew.

Sally linked Vicky by the arm. 'You beat me at football last time we met,' she said to Danny. '*This* time, I'm *not* going to be on the losing side.' She smiled dangerously, and with a swish of her bright red pigtails flounced out of the wigwam.

Welly Wars

Everyone returned to the Wygol-y-wigwam for lunch. Danny pulled off his muddy wellingtons, dropped them in the boys' boot zone by the entrance and scurried inside. He kept his head down while he ate his lamb stew and Welsh cakes, in case Sally Butterworth tried to embarrass him again.

'Where's Silly Bottyburp?' asked Matthew, gazing around the enormous tent. 'She's not here. What's she up to?'

'If we're lucky, she's been captured by aliens and taken to the planet Zigga-bigga-fafa-iggy-dig 9,' replied Danny.

At that moment he spotted Sally's bright red pigtails as she sauntered back into the wigwam.

'No such luck,' he said, ducking down again. 'She's just been to the Pee-pee Teepees!'

The lunch bowls were collected, and Bush blew hard on his duck whistle. QUACK!

QUAAAAAAACK!

'First to get to the woodland bottom-shuffling course gets a point for their team! Look lively!'

The kids charged through the tunnel and headed for their boots.

'Where's my welly?' demanded Danny, seeing that he only had one boot.

'And mine?' said Matthew.

'And mine?' chorused the other boys.

'There they are!' shouted Danny's classmate Jimmy Sedgley, pointing to the roof of the boys' hut. It was strewn with the missing wellingtons.

'The Welsh Welly Fairies must have flung them up there while you were eating,' suggested Sally, charging off into the forest with the rest of the girls.

'That's not fair!' said Danny, pulling on his single boot and hopping after her. The other boys did the same, but they didn't stand a chance, and the girls easily won the race.

Danny looked at the fed-up faces of the other boys as they lined up for the woodland bottom-shuffle relay. 'Come on, lads,' he urged. 'Let's show those cheating girls who's best!'

The boys bottom-shuffled as hard as they could, weaving between trees and rocks along the twisting, bumpy course, but the girls shuffled harder and once again were victorious.

'I told you,' taunted Sally. 'This time, *I'm* going to be on the winning team!'

As the kids made their way back through the woods to the huts, Danny spied some gloopy frog spawn bobbing stickily at the edge of a shallow pond, and a wicked idea popped into his head.

'Where can I get a bucket?' he said to Matt.

That evening the kids returned to the Wygol-y-wigwam for supper and sing-song.

'Save me a place, Matt,' said Danny. 'I need to go to the Pee-pee Teepees.'

The clearing was deserted. Danny saw the rows of wellington boots lined up outside, boys on the left, girls on the right. He dashed round to the back of the boys' hut where he'd hidden a bucket of frog spawn. Danny slopped a dollop of the gloopy jelly-eggs into each of the girls' wellingtons and hurried back to supper.

'The naughty Welsh Welly Fairies have been up to their tricks again,' he whispered to Matthew, tucking into a Welsh spicy sausage.

After supper and singing the camp song, Bunny announced, 'Time for bed, kids! Ladies first!'

85

Danny held his breath.

Bunny led the girls out of the wigwam and the boys hurried out after them. Danny heard the lovely squelch and squish as the unsuspecting girls shoved their feet into their frogspawny boots.

Sally Butterworth stormed up to Danny, frog eggs dripping down the sides of her wellingtons.

'You!' she yelled.

'Me!' he laughed.

'This means WAR!' declared Sally.

'Bring it on!' grinned Danny.

Tickety-boo!

Poo-wiggly-wig Adventure Centre
Wales

Silly-billy-dilly-dally-bing-bang-bong, Mr Bibby!

That's the Poo-wiggly-wig greeting! Guess what?
Sally Butterworth's here. She's *still* going on
about that yucky kissing world record we set in
Spain, and she's still mad about her team losing
the football match against us, and the row we
had about her jelly-lips wrecking my Mexican
Jelly-wave.

We were out in the woods
yesterday doing a woodland
bottom-shuffle relay race.
When we woke up this morning,
everyone was covered with
Snowdonian Tiger Ticks. They're

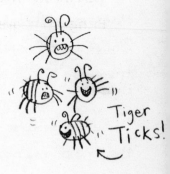

Tiger
Ticks!

little stripy orange-and-black balls with short
wriggly legs. Bush Tucker, the boys' leader, is a
bug expert. He says ticks stick their long pointy
mouths under your skin and suck out your blood
until they pop and let loose zillions of babies.
Ace!

We've been quarantined, which means we've got
to stay for an extra two weeks. Mega Ace! The
whole camp's got to be fumigated. We've got to
be fumigated!

Bunny Grylls — the girls' leader —
pulled the ticks off the kids with
'Bunny's Non-pop Non-stop
Humane Tick-plucker'. Then
Matthew and Vicky Wilmott
(Sally's best friend) counted
them.

Sally
(yuck!)
her friend
Vicky

I had eighty-nine ticks, including one right on
the end of my nose, but Sally Butterworth

had 577. Thanks to her, the girls won *that* competition, 4,567 to 3,112.

I know she likes breaking records too, so I was wondering: is Tiger-ticky Sally a world-beater?

Best wishes
Danny Baker

PS Josh Davis bottom-shuffled on to a big pine cone near the end of the race and had to go to hospital to have it removed. He's kept it as a souvenir.

Pine-cone bum

The Great Big Book
of World Records
London

ARE YOU A RECORD
BREAKER ?

Dear Danny

Woodland Bottom-shuffling is fun, isn't it? It
originated in the rainforests of Cameroon and
was brought back to Wales in the nineteenth
century by Jones Owen-Jones, an explorer from
St Melons. The BedPan tribe of pygmies had a
genetic condition that gave them constantly
itchy bottoms, and the only way they could get
relief was to shuffle around the forest floor.
Sadly, it made them easy prey for leopards, and
the tribe is now extinct.

With regard to Sally Butterworth's ticks:
I am delighted to tell you that she is a
record breaker. She has easily broken the
previous world record for Total-body Tiger-
tick Infestation, which was held by tick-boffin

Dr Ellie Doo. As a matter of interest, Dr Doo explored the Congo in the hope of collecting as many different species of tick on her body as possible. She had 433 individual creatures, from fourteen separate species, stuck on her body, and even discovered one – Tyrannotickus rex – that was previously unknown to science. Unfortunately it was as big as a dinner plate, and in less than an hour had sucked all four litres of blood from her body, including the blood the other 432 ticks had gobbled, killing poor Dr Doo and her entire collection of ticks. So think yourselves lucky it was just the Snowdonian Tiger Tick that had a chew on you!

I have enclosed Sally's certificate. Would you kindly pass it on to her?

Best wishes
Eric Bibby
Keeper of the Records

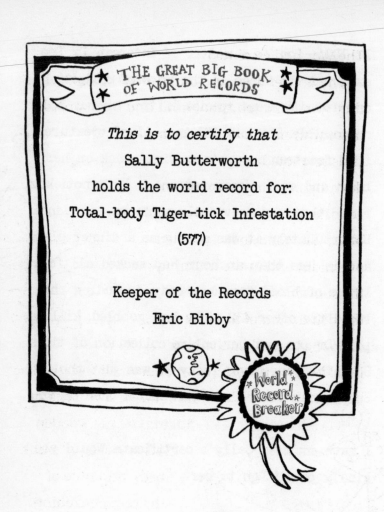

THE GREAT BIG BOOK OF WORLD RECORDS

This is to certify that
Sally Butterworth
holds the world record for:
Total-body Tiger-tick Infestation
(577)

Keeper of the Records
Eric Bibby

World Record Breaker

The War had escalated.

The Bonzer Boys had ambushed the girls while they were on a toadstool hunt and bombarded them with mudballs. The Gobsmacking Girls retaliated when it went dark, by planting Trumphorn Toadstools in the boys' shower block. The toadstools sprouted overnight and in the morning the showers were heavy with the rich aroma of fungusy farts.

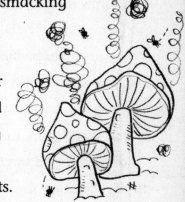

So the boys filled the girls' lunchboxes with worms, woodlice and weevils. The girls got their own back by taking out the wooden slats in the boys' bunk beds, and nine of the boys, including Danny, had fallen through and got stuck. But Danny was planning an attack of his own, and everything was ready . . .

It had been over an hour since the loud, twangy sound of the Curfew Kazoo had echoed through the camp and lights had been turned out. Danny had kept himself awake making up his own version of the Camp Song:

'Always trump when you are windy,

If you don't you'll surely cry.

Never wash when you are dirty,

And you'll stink up to the sky!'

Soon he heard the rasp of Bush Tucker's snores ripping through the darkness like a pig with a sore throat. Danny swung his legs over the edge of the bunk bed, lowering himself down until he felt his bare feet touch the edge of Matthew's bed, then the floor.

Matt was sleeping soundly, his hair poking out from beneath his duvet. Danny prodded him awake.

'Silly-Sally-dolly-belly-bong-bang-bing!' he whispered. 'Fancy a midnight raid on the girls' hut?'

Matthew rubbed his eyes. 'Dippy-dappy-soppy-

Sally-ding-dang-dong,' he mumbled. 'To do what?'

Danny reached under the bed and slid out a long, flat cardboard box with the words 'Pritchard's Pilchards' printed down the sides. He carefully opened the lid, shining his torch inside for Matt to see. The box was criss-crossed with threads of flimsy silver webs, and swarmed with hundreds of hairy black spiders.

'I wondered where all the spiders in the hut had disappeared to,' said Matthew.

'I've been collecting them,' Danny explained. 'There's another boxful under the bed. I thought the girls would like to have them in *their* hut.'

Matthew grinned. 'Count me in!' he hissed, sliding from under the duvet.

Danny pulled out the second box of spiders and

handed it to Matt. The two boys grabbed their wellington boots and tiptoed silently to the door. The key turned in the lock with a loud click. The boys froze, waiting for Bush's voice to boom at them, but only his snores disturbed the silence. They crept out into the black night.

A soft wind tugged at their pyjamas and made the trees whisper warnings in the darkness. 'Don't do it!' they seemed to hiss. 'You'll be sorry!'

The boys slipped their boots on, straining their eyes to peer into the night for Llewellyn and guard-goose Gwyneth. The camp seemed deserted.

'Come on,' whispered Danny. 'Stick to the shadows and keep your ears open.'

They skirted around the edge of the camp and past the Pee-pee Teepees, until they reached the girls' hut.

Danny spotted that the door to the hut was slightly ajar. He eased it open a few centimetres and the boys carefully tipped the hairy spiders out. The creatures scurried away into the dark, silent dormitory.

'Mission accomplished!' whispered Danny.
'Return to base!'

As they turned to make their way back, they heard a loud honking bark coming from the trees.

HONK! HONK! HONK! HONK! HONK!

'Intruders is it, Gwyneth?' hissed Llewellyn's voice in the darkness nearby.

'Oh no!' gasped Matthew. 'We're goose-food!'

Danny thought fast. He pushed Matthew back into the shadows. 'Get back to our hut when the coast's clear! I'll cause a diversion,' he said, then dashed out into the clearing in front of the Wygol-y-wigwam, to trip the security sensors.

Four floodlights snapped on, dazzling Danny with intense white light. He screwed his eyes tight shut, and when he opened them again, Sally Butterworth stood in front of him wearing red pyjamas and purple wellington boots.

'Silly-Sally-dilly-dally-bing-bang-bong!' said Danny. 'What are you doing here?'

'Dopey-Danny-dilly-dally-bing-bang-bong!' replied Sally, looking as surprised as he was.

'What are *you* doing here?'

'Just out for a stroll,' he replied.

They glared at each other suspiciously. Sally opened her mouth to say something else, but stopped as what Danny thought must be the biggest, ugliest, gruesomest goose in the world waddled out of the darkness. Its wings were spread out and its long neck stretched forward in an attack position.

HONK! HONK! HONK! HONK! HONK!

Sally huddled close to Danny, and grabbed his arm.

'G-g-good g-g-goosey,' he stammered.

Gwyneth marched

towards them, honking loudly.

'Doesn't understand English, my Gwyneth,' chuckled Llewellyn the security guard, looming out of the darkness behind the goose, 'only Welsh.'

Danny gulped. 'What's Welsh for "Silly-billy-dilly-dally-bing-bang-bong"?' he asked Sally.

'I think that *is* Welsh,' she replied.

Luckily, at that moment, Bush and Bunny ran from their huts to see what had caused the commotion.

'Caught these two snooping around after Lights Out, we did,' said Llewellyn, calling Gwyneth to heel and slipping a lead around her neck. The goose honked once at Danny and Sally, fixing them with her beady yellow eyes.

'I'm sorry, you two,' said Bush. 'You know the rules. You're gonna have to do the Poo-wiggly-wig Wipe-up: scrape off the sloppy leftovers from every meal, and wash up the dish mountain!'

Sally turned and glared at Danny. 'Now look what you've done!' she snapped.

'You started it, Buttyworm!' he replied.

Bunny Grylls wagged her finger at him. 'Now that's no way to speak to your girlfriend,' she said.

Danny growled with frustration. 'SHE'S . . . NOT . . . MY . . . GIRLFRIEND!'

Flea-bitten

Next morning, the Wakey-wakey Hooter parped through the forest, blasting the campers from their sweet dreams. It stopped, and for a moment there was silence in the camp. Then shrill shrieks from the girls' hut sliced through the peace and quiet.

Danny hung upside down from his bunk bed, grinning at Matthew.

'In. The. Net!' he said, dropping to the floor and hurrying outside. 'The Bonzer Boys are on the scoreboard!'

The boys spilt out into the courtyard to see what was happening as a stream

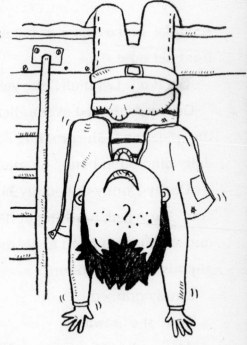

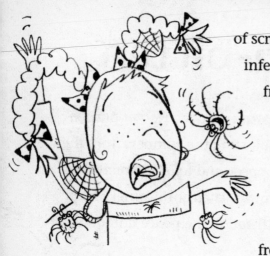

of screaming, spider-infested girls barged from their hut.

Sally Butterworth burst through the door. A delicate silver web stretched from her ear to her shoulder, and a spider as big as a biscuit swung from her nose.

'Get it off! Get it off!' she yelled.

Danny sauntered over to her and gently lifted the spider on to the ground. 'Soppy-Sally-dilly-dally-bing-bang-bong,' he said.

'Dopey-Danny-dilly-dally-bing-bang-bong to you!' she yelled, brushing at her arms and legs and shaking her head to get any spiders out of her pigtails. 'With knobs on!'

Danny grinned.

'You!' she growled.

'Me!' replied Danny, scratching his left armpit.

Vicky Wilmott strolled over to them. 'Silly-billy-dilly-dally-bing-bang-bong, Matt,' she said. Her head was enveloped in a shining cap of silvery webs, and the dozen tiny spiders that had spun them.

'Silly-billy-dilly-dally-bing-bang-bong, Vicky,' Matthew replied, scratching his tummy. 'Your hair looks cool.'

'Thanks. I like spiders.'

'*They* don't,' said Danny, grinning at a group of girls who seemed to be doing a strange dance, running round in circles, screeching wildly and waving their arms about their heads.

'Don't be soft, girls!' said Bunny Grylls, wading into the hysterical mob. 'At least they're not poisonous like the ones back home. On my first trip into the Australian outback, I woke up one morning covered in deadly Burrumbuttock Bottom-biter spiders. I had to sit on a wombat for three days to neutralize the effects of the venom!'

Danny rubbed his elbow, then scraped at his knee. He noticed Matthew standing on one leg to scratch his toes. Six or seven of the other boys from his hut were scratching themselves furiously.

'I've got fleas!' cried Jimmy Sedgley.

Danny glared at Sally. 'You!'

'Me!' she answered. 'That makes us even!'

Bush picked one of the fleas off Jimmy and examined the insect closely. 'Holy Dooley! This is the Snowdonian Fidgeting Flea,' he said. 'These little beauties produce five-hundred and sixty-nine flea-babies every hour! It's no wonder you're all crawling. They make you itch like blazes!'

Bush rubbed his chin thoughtfully. 'These

bities usually live on the Lesser-warty Woodland Hedgehog. I wonder . . .'

He went into the boys' hut and emerged a minute later with a family of spiky and not-too-warty hedgehogs in a cardboard box. 'Just as I thought: I found these little fellas snuffling around under your beds,' he said. '*That's* why you're all jumping with fleas.'

'Competition time!' said Bunny. 'Who's the most infested, boys or girls? Matt, Vicky, get counting!'

'Fab!' cried Vicky.

'Cool!' agreed Matthew.

Bush turned to Danny and Sally. 'Don't forget, you two: from today, and for the rest of the week, you're doing the Poo-wiggly-wig Wipe-up: scrape up the slops and wash the dish mountain!'

'Bet I can slop and wash more dishes than you,' scowled Sally.

'There's only one way to find out,' replied Danny. 'Go for your dishcloth!'

Mucky Pups

Poo-wiggly-wig Adventure Centre
Wales

Dear Mr Bibby

This place is Bug Central! I managed to collect
1,899 spiders, and me and Matt let them loose in
the girls' hut last night. They were not happy.

The girls had the last laugh though, because
Sally Butterworth hid some flea-infested
hedgehogs in *our* hut, and this morning every
one of us was covered with fleas. Matt and
his new friend Vicky
Wilmott counted a
total of 22,371 fleas
on all the boys. Jimmy
Sedgley had 18,423
all to himself. Our

hedgehog
and fleas!

spider

Leader, Bush Tucker, says Jimmy must have very tasty blood.

We've all been fumigated again. Ace! Jimmy was wondering if he had broken a world record with his flea-count, so I said I'd ask you.

Best wishes
Danny Baker

ARE YOU A RECORD
BREAKER ?

Dear Danny

You can pass on the good news to Jimmy Sedgley
that he has broken the world record for
Individual Flea Infestation, previously held
by American magician and illusionist David
Chill-Blaine. In 2005, Mr Chill-Blaine stood
for ten days, sixteen hours, forty-two minutes
and eleven seconds, in a locked glass box in
Trafalgar Square while 15,941 South Korean
Fighting Fleas nibbled at his body. Amazingly,
he didn't scratch once.

Eventually he was forced to come out when the
glass tank he was standing in got so covered in
pigeon droppings that no one could see him any
more.

Was it a trick? Doctors appointed by the Great
Big Book of World Records checked his skin.
They found no reason to disqualify him from
claiming the record for Individual Flea
Infestation, which Jimmy Sedgley has now
broken.

Mr Chill-Blaine does still hold the Flea-induced
Itch-resistance world record.

Would you please pass on Jimmy's certificate
and my congratulations!

Best wishes
Eric Bibby
Keeper of the Records

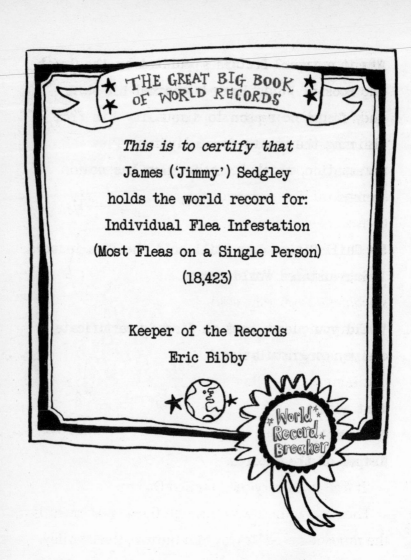

THE GREAT BIG BOOK OF WORLD RECORDS

This is to certify that
James ('Jimmy') Sedgley
holds the world record for:
Individual Flea Infestation
(Most Fleas on a Single Person)
(18,423)

Keeper of the Records
Eric Bibby

World Record Breaker

After a breakfast of cockles and bacon, and cheese on toast, Danny and Sally had finished doing the slops and dish mountain for the third day in a row, and stood looking at the Cool Competition scoreboard. The Gobsmacking Girls were way ahead of the Bonzer Boys.

Sally grinned. 'Wow! We're *slaughtering* you,' she said.

Danny nodded. '*And* everyone seems to be getting records, except me.'

'It's not everyone – just me and Jimmy.'

'It *feels* like everyone,' replied Danny.

They made their way through the woods towards the mudslide area. It was in a narrow, steep valley, and the boys had set up on one side of the stream, the girls on the other.

'See you at the Supper Sing-song, Dan,' said

Sally, climbing the steep slope towards the girls.

Danny scampered up to join Matthew, who was smoothing a gloopy patch of mud down with his hands.

'Dippy-dappy-soppy-Sally-ding-dang-dong, Dan!' said his friend. 'Did you beat Salty Buttybum at the brekkie slops and dish mountain today?'

'Silly-Sally-dolly-belly-bong-bang-bing, Matt' replied Danny. 'No, she won by a teaspoon.' He looked at the mudslide. 'How's it going?'

'Pretty good. We've got to make a curly-wurly slide that spells out a word, and see how many kids we can get to slide to the last letter,' explained Matthew. 'We're spelling "gastro-enteritis".'

Danny looked across the valley at the girls' effort. It was already longer than the boys', and had lots of l's and w's and y's in it. 'That's not a proper word.'

'Vicky says it's a place in Wales, and she should know, she's half Welsh.'

'Which half?'

Matthew shrugged. 'The top half, I suppose,' he

replied. 'She can play football, so her legs *must* be English!'

Danny joined in making the slide. When it was complete, the boys took turns to sit on a tea-tray and hurtle down and around the wet, muddy letters. It was great until they got halfway down, when the tea-tray clunked over a bump, throwing each rider into the shallow stream running along the bottom of the valley.

The girls had planned it better. They had got the angle right and made the mud so slippery that the tea-tray rocketed down the slide, off the end of the word, and skipped along for four or five metres.

'Spiffy! The Gobsmacking Girls win again!' cheered Bunny Grylls. 'That's the longest mudslide word I've ever seen!'

'I'll go and ask Vicky if she'd like to measure it with me,' said Matthew, setting off down the slope.

'Matt . . .' called Danny, but his friend had already dashed over to where Vicky stood.

Danny joined the queue to have a go on the girls' mudslide. He sat down on a rotting fallen tree trunk and soon felt something tickle his ankle. He glanced down and saw a line of ants hurrying up his trouser leg. There was a nest in the rotting log, and Danny was sitting on top of it!

'Ace!' he said, mesmerized by the long lines of tiny brown creatures scurrying to and from the nest. The ants climbing up his leg had reached his bottom . . .

Danny began to wiggle.

Then he began to squiggle.

Soon he began to jiggle.

'Mega Ace!' he laughed.

'What's the matter, Danny?' asked Bush. 'Have you got ants in your pants?'

'Yeah!' replied Danny truthfully.

'I think you're the Cheekiest Scamp in the Camp, young fella!' said Bush as Danny wiggled, squiggled and jiggled away, furiously scratching his itchy bottom.

Ants in His Pants

Poo-wiggly-wig Adventure Centre
Wales

Dear Mr Bibby

Yesterday, the girls made an Ace mudslide, and spelled out the word:

Llanfairpwllgwyngyllgogerychwyrndrobwllllantysilio-gogogoch.

It was 73.67 m long, and was so greasy and skiddy that everyone managed to get from the first letter to the last! The girls' leader said it was the longest mudslide word

mudslide!

she had ever seen. Did they break the world record?

Best wishes
Danny Baker

PS I got a few ants in my pants yesterday, but I couldn't keep them there. When they got a whiff of the Welsh cakes cooking for supper, they were off! What's the longest time anyone has ever survived having ants in their pants? I'm going to give it a go!

Dear Danny

I'm delighted to tell you that the girls
have broken the world record for Mudslide
Lexicography (Mud Writing!) with their fifty-
eight-letter attempt.

'Llanfairpwllgwyngyllgogerychwyrndrobwllllantysiliogogogoch' smashed the previous record
by twenty letters! This was held by thirty-one
members of the obscure Docduc tribe on one
of the smaller islands in Papua New Guinea.
In 1988 they formed their own Mary Poppins
Appreciation Society, in the belief that this
magical lady was a goddess who would one day
fly in to their village holding an umbrella,
teach them to sing nice songs, and keep their
bedrooms tidy.

Inspired by the song with a similar title, they created a mudslide of the word 'soppycollyfroggylickytickyolliedocious'. Sadly they didn't know how to spell the original word, and it lost something in translation. However, it gained something too: four extra letters!

I'm glad to hear you are attempting a record, Danny. I seem to be sending certificates to everyone else in your Adventure Camp except you! The Ant-filled Underwear Endurance world record is one of the hardest to break. By an extraordinary coincidence, this record is also held by someone from a tribe in Papua New Guinea. When the time comes to choose a new leader, the men of the tribe fill their loincloths with ferocious Melanesian Mango-muncher Ants and see who can keep his loincloth on for the longest. In 1957 Zun Bako gritted his teeth and kept his composure for six hours, fourteen minutes and forty-seven seconds, but

because of the numerous bites to his behind was
unable to sit down ever again.

My advice would be to choose a species of
vegetarian ant that won't want to bite your
bottom! Good luck!

Best wishes
Eric Bibby
Keeper of the Records

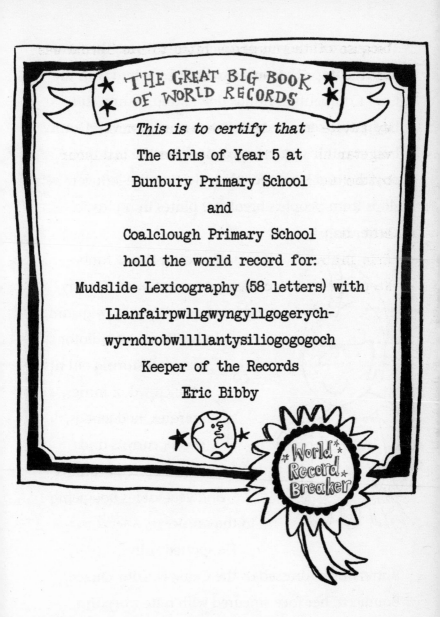

THE GREAT BIG BOOK OF WORLD RECORDS

This is to certify that
The Girls of Year 5 at
Bunbury Primary School
and
Coalclough Primary School
hold the world record for:
Mudslide Lexicography (58 letters) with
Llanfairpwllgwyngyllgogerych-
wyrndrobwllllantysiliogogogoch
Keeper of the Records
Eric Bibby

World Record Breaker

The quarantine was at an end and it was the final day at camp. The Gobsmacking Girls had won the Cool Competition hands down, and Danny still hadn't broken a record. It was now or never: Danny had to put his plan into action. For the last three days he had been secretly collecting the leftover slops from people's breakfast plates in a plastic carrier bag.

It was the Going Home fancy-dress tea-party and disco. Danny stood inside the Wygol-y-wigwam in his Roman gladiator costume, staring out at the crowd of fairies, pirates, hedgehogs, sheep, carrots and other assorted animals and vegetables boogieing to the music.

He spotted Sally Butterworth, dressed as the Celtic warrior Queen Boudicca, her face smeared with blue warpaint, glaring at him from the far side of the room. Clearly the War was not over.

Danny sidled up to a pair of calculators standing together by the pop-bottle table. Matthew and Vicky's faces grinned at him from the place where the screens would be.

'Silly-billy-dilly-dally-bing-bang-bong, Vicky,' he said.

'Silly-billy-dilly-dally-bing-bang-bong, Danny,' replied Vicky.

'I'm just going outside,' he whispered to Matthew. 'I may be some time. If anyone asks where I am, say I've gone to the Pee-pee Teepees.'

'Where *are* you going?' asked Matt.

'To get ants in my pants,' replied Danny.

He sneaked out of the wigwam and hurried over to the boys' hut to collect his slop bag of ant bait from under the bunk bed.

It was still daylight, and he made his way quickly through the trees towards the ants' nest. When he got there, he lifted his short leather gladiator skirt and began to stuff the leftover food into his underpants. In no time, the pants bulged with:

four half-eaten strawberry-jam sandwiches

one green, mouldy cheese-and-pickle sandwich

three splattered egg-and-ketchup sandwiches

two squashed Welsh cakes

a squishy, black, rotten banana

a greasy lamb chop

six slices of limp, wet tomato

three chicken drumsticks in sticky barbecue
    sauce

four green-pepper-
    and-onion
    pizza slices

nine spat-out
    pieces of
    Welsh spicy
    sausage

fifteen cold chips

a slice of slimy laver bread

a splodge of gooseberry yogurt

a blob of rhubarb crumble (with custard)

and

a couple of cockles.

Danny stared at the seething mass of insects
swarming around the rotten
log and asked himself, 'Do
I *really* want to put my
bottom in that lot?'

He thought about
it for a moment.
'Yeah, I do!'

He sat down
with a squelch in
the middle of the ants'
nest. 'Grub's up! Come
and get it!'

The smell wafting from Danny's pants was
irresistible to the tiny creatures. They instantly
swarmed up his legs and into his underpants. It felt

as though his bottom was being tickled by a trillion tiny feet which, Danny realized, it was.

Danny wiggled slowly back to the camp. The itching on his bottom was agonizing as the ants went into a feeding frenzy on the food plastered in his pants. He crept back into the wigwam and stood by the door with Matthew, twitching and wriggling.

Bunny Grylls danced over to the boys. 'What's the matter, Danny?' she asked. 'Have you got ants in your pants?'

'Yeah! I have!' replied Danny through gritted teeth.

'Ripper!' laughed Bunny. 'I once camped in the rainforests on the Zamboanga Peninsula and got bats in my hats!' she told him. 'And when I was trying to save a pond near Grimsby I got coots in my boots!'

'And her brain down the drain!' whispered Danny as Bunny boogied away.

Matthew coughed as he tried not to laugh.

The intense prickling on Danny's bottom and

legs was unbearable. The ants were *really* on the move.

Sally 'Boudicca' Butterworth stormed up to him and pointed her floppy cardboard spear at his chest. Danny pulled out his plastic sword and batted it away.

'Where've you been?' she demanded. 'What've you been up to?'

Danny couldn't stand still so he pretended to dance. 'Just been for a stroll,' he replied.

The music finished and DJ Bush Tucker announced that supper was served: 'Grub's up, cobbers!'

Sally thrust her spear into the air, put back her head and let out a loud wailing battle cry.

'Ee-yiy-yay-eeeeeeeeeeeeeeeeeeeee!

Gobsmacking Girls to the buffet!
Chaaaaaaaaaaaaaaaaarge!'

At Sally's signal the girls stormed the buffet
table, attacking the platters of food, stuffing
handfuls of sandwiches, cakes and sausage rolls
into pockets and pants.
Before the boys knew
what was happening,
the table was
empty and the
girls' costumes
swelled with piles
of pillaged food.
Boudicca
Butterworth stood
in front of the girl
army and let out her
triumphant battle cry once more.

'Ee-yiy-yay-eeeeeeeeeeeeeeeeeeeeee! Victory! The
Gobsmacking Girls win again!'

Danny stomped up to her, and the boys closed
ranks behind him, lining up against the girls. The

two groups
stood
glaring at
each other.

'That's
not fair!' he
snapped.

'All's fair in love
and war, my mum says,' replied Sally.

'This battle isn't over yet,' said Danny, standing
eye to eye with Sally.

Suddenly, he felt the ants leaving his pants
and spreading down his legs. He realized at once
where they were going. Danny continued to glare
at Sally until she began to twitch. He grinned as

a wave of wiggling,
squiggling and
jiggling spread
through the
crowd of girls
like ripples
across a

pond, as the ants swarmed into their pockets and pants in search of more food to eat.

'What's the matter with you girls?' asked Bush. 'Have you *all* got ants in your pants?'

'Yes!' they cried. 'Argggghhhhhhh! Get them out! Get them out!'

Danny turned to Matthew. 'My record attempt finished as soon as it started,' he said. 'But I don't care! The Bonzer Boys have won the war!'

Bush Tucker scooped up a handful of the tiny creatures scurrying across the floor.

'These are Rotty-log Restless Roaming Ants,' he announced. 'They're always on the hunt for bonzer tucker. By tomorrow the whole camp could be infested.'

Sally waved her floppy spear at Danny once again. 'Get these ants out of our pants!'

He shrugged. 'It's your own fault,' he reminded

her. 'You pinched all the food.'

Bunny laughed. 'Fair dinkum, girls,' she said. 'You're getting your comeuppance.'

Danny grabbed the tablecloth and dropped it on the floor. 'The ants are after the food,' he said to the girls. 'Chuck it all on to there.'

They did as Danny asked, and immediately long lines of ants began to stream down legs, heading straight for their supper. Danny folded over the four corners of the tablecloth, and slung it over his shoulder.

'Good on ya, Danny!' cried Bush. 'That's gotta be the world's biggest tucker bag!'

'Take the little bities back where they came from,' said Bunny.

'We'll come with you,' said Matthew.

Danny strolled out of the wigwam and through the woods, like the Pied Piper of Hamelin, leading the long string of ants out of the camp. Matthew, Sally and Vicky walked by his side, singing the camp song, including Danny's naughty version.

When they reached the nest, he dropped the sack

of food on to the ground next to the log and stood back, waiting for the insects to catch up.

'What's that noise?' asked Vicky.

HONK! HONK! HONK! HONK! HONK!

'It's Llewellyn and Gwyneth!' replied Matthew.

The security guard and his goose crashed out of the forest. Gwyneth hissed angrily at the children.

'Silly-billy-dilly-dally-bing-bang-bong,' said Llewellyn, laughing at the strange group in front of him. 'Now, I ask myself, what would a Roman gladiator, a Celtic warrior and two calculators be doing out in the forest alone?'

'Picnic,' said Danny, opening the tablecloth to show him the food.

The goose lunged towards it.

'Gwyneth!' roared Llewellyn, but the big bird yanked hard on her lead, and tugged him over into the pile of food, gobbling greedily at a cheese-and-tomato sandwich.

At that moment, the ants arrived.

Gwyneth gave a short, loud 'HONK!' and began to wiggle.

Llewellyn gasped and began to squiggle.

Then they both began to jiggle.

'What's going on?' asked the security guard.

'You've got ants in your pants!' chorused Danny, Matthew, Sally and Vicky.

Gruesome guard-goose Gwyneth charged off down the valley, honking loudly and dragging Llewellyn after her. She skidded on to the girls' mudslide and the pair of them slid off along Llanfairpwllgwyngyllgogerychwyrndrobwllllantysiliogogogoch. A shower of rain that morning had freshened up the slimy slope and they zoomed along the muddy word, swirling and twirling gracefully towards the stream at the bottom.

'GWYNEEEEEEEEEEEEEEEEETH!
STOOOOOOOOOOOOOOOOOOOP!'

SPLASH!

The kids high-fived.

'Mission accomplished!' laughed Danny. He held out his hand towards Sally. 'Truce?' he asked.

'Truce,' agreed Sally, shaking his hand. 'Let's go home.'

Danny Baker
Record Breaker

Poo-wiggly-wig Adventure Centre
Wales

G'day Mr Bibby (That's 'hello' in Australian)

I couldn't beat the Ant-filled Underwear
Endurance world record, but I did manage to
infect fifty-three people and one goose with
the ants from my pants. Bunny Grylls, the girls'
leader, says she's certain
this is a world record. I
hope this is true, because
I feel left out – almost
everyone else has
broken a record these
last three weeks except me!

my pants!

ants

We're leaving Poo-wiggly-wig today. It's been Ace, but I'm looking forward to getting my football boots on again and playing footy.

And I miss my sister Natalie – not!

Best wishes
Danny Baker

'You stink!' said Mum, when Danny walked into the house at the end of the trip. 'Have you had a bath or a shower *at all* while you've been away?'

'I didn't need to,' he replied. 'I was only away three weeks.'

Danny opened his suitcase and tipped it upside down next to the washing machine. His dirty clothes slid out and landed with a wet splat, spraying mud and dirty water across the

floor. A beetle, three woodlice, four centipedes and

a spider scuttled from underneath the grubby mound.

'I hope you haven't brought any more wildlife home,' said Mum, shaking her head as she surveyed the muddy mess on the floor.

'Here's one,' said Dad, picking an earwig from Danny's left ear.

Danny handed Natalie something big and rectangular-shaped wrapped in plain brown paper. 'I got you a present, Nat.'

His sister narrowed her eyes. 'Is it poisonous? Will it give me a rash?'

'It's educational,' replied Danny.

Natalie carefully unwrapped the present, revealing a shallow wooden box with a glass front. The inside of the box was divided up into square sections, each containing different-sized brown or black balls. Her face crumpled in disgust.

'It's a box of poo!' she exclaimed.

'It's a *display* box of *Welsh Mountain* Poo,' corrected Danny, pointing out some of the sections. 'That shiny poo's from a Snowdonian

Shuffling Short-haired Sheep. The hairy poo's from a Bryn Ballybont Burping Badger. The sloppy poo's from a Wild Woodland Chuckling Chicken. This sausage-y poo's from a Tallypant Vampire Mole. And that specky poo's from a . . .'

'This is the world's worst present!' cried Natalie, thrusting the box back into Danny's hands.

'Don't you like it?' he asked, trying not to laugh.

'Keep your smelly present!' replied his sister, storming out of the room.

'I knew I should have got her a stick of rock,' grinned Danny.

ARE YOU A RECORD
BREAKER ?

Dear Danny

Fantastic! You've done it again! You have
broken the world record for Single-handed
Ant-in-pant Multiple-person (and Animal) Ant
Infestation. Coincidentally, Bunny Grylls
was the previous record holder. In 2003 she
accidentally spread an ant infestation of her
pants to thirty-nine archaeologists she was
leading through the Mexican jungle to study
the lost Aztec city of Pippapoppapeppapootle.

I am delighted to enclose yet another
certificate for your collection.

Good on ya, Danny! (That means 'Well done' in
Australian.)

140

Best wishes

Eric Bibby

Keeper of the Records

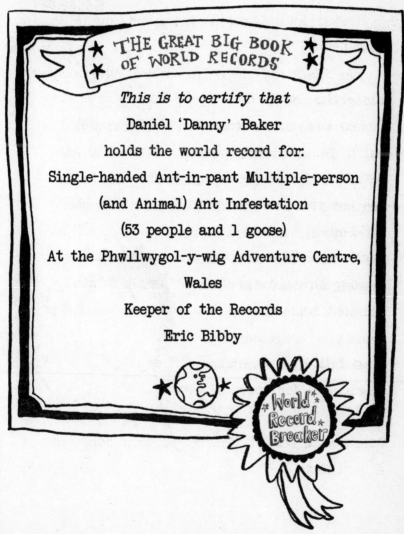

THE GREAT BIG BOOK OF WORLD RECORDS

This is to certify that

Daniel 'Danny' Baker

holds the world record for:

Single-handed Ant-in-pant Multiple-person

(and Animal) Ant Infestation

(53 people and 1 goose)

At the Phwllwygol-y-wig Adventure Centre,

Wales

Keeper of the Records

Eric Bibby

World Record Breaker

Matthew stood by Danny's bed and studied the box of animal droppings hanging on the wall next to Danny's collection of world-record certificates.

'Didn't Nat the Brat like her present then?' he asked.

'No,' laughed Danny. 'She's weird. Who *wouldn't* want a box of poo?'

Danny rummaged under his bed and pulled out a jam-jar containing a slice of slimy Welsh laver bread. A seething mass of Rotty-log Restless Roaming Ants swarmed all over it, nibbling and chewing their seaweed supper.

'It's lucky I brought home something else for her,' he grinned. 'She might not want poo on her wall, but she's sure to want ants in her pants!'

THE WORLD'S
BIGGEST BOGEY

STEVE HARTLEY

TO THE MANAGER
The Great Big Book
of World Records
London

Dear Sir,
I have been collecting
bogeys from my nose for the
last two years.
I have stuck them all together
to make one enormous bogey. It
measures 5.3 cm in diameter and
weighs 3.6 grams. Is this a record?

Yours faithfully,

Danny Baker

(Aged nine and a bit)

WARNING!
THIS STORY
MAY CONTAIN
SILLINESS

Join Danny as he attempts to smash a
load of revolting records, including:

LOUDEST TRUMP!
CHEESIEST FEET!
NITTIEST SCALP!

OUT NOW!

THE WORLD'S
AWESOMEST AIR-BARF

STEVE HARTLEY

TO THE MANAGER
The Great Big Book
of World Records
London

Dear Sir,
I flew to Spain yesterday
and I filled thirteen sick-bags
on the flight. Mum says it was all
the cola and cheese and pickle
sandwiches I had at the airport.
She's right – that's why I had them!
Is this even close to breaking the
record for filling sick-bags? If it's
not, I'll try again on the way home.

Yours faithfully,
Danny Baker
(Aged nine and a half)

WARNING!
NOT TO BE
READ AT
MEALTIMES

**Join Danny as he attempts to smash a
load of hilarious records, including:**

FRECKLIEST FACE!
PONGIEST POTION!
SQUELCHIEST COWPATS!

OUT NOW!

THE WORLD'S
LOUDEST ARMPIT FART

STEVE HARTLEY

TO THE MANAGER
The Great Big Book
of World Records
London

Dear Sir,
Yesterday I attempted
the Continuous Musical Armpit-
farting record. I managed to play
2081 verses of 'Old MacDonald Had a
Farm' before I squeezed too hard
and bruised my fingers.
My sister was upstairs, trying to listen
to her favourite boy band. Even with
the volume turned right up she could
still hear my armpit farts! Could they
have been the Loudest Ever?
Yours faithfully,
Danny Baker
(Aged nine and three quarters)

WARNING!
COVER
YOUR
EARS!

Join Danny as he attempts to smash a
load of crazy records, including:

MESSIEST JELLY FIGHT!
CRINKLIEST WRINKLES!
VILEST VERRUCAS!

OUT NOW!

THE WORLD'S
STICKIEST EARWAX

STEVE HARTLEY

TO THE MANAGER
The Great Big Book
of World Records
London

Dear Sir,
I'm making a model of
the Carnival Parade for an art
project at school - out of earwax!
If you look closely, you can see the 159
spectators (including my mum and dad).
My mates have been giving me their
ear-goo for months and I've been
keeping it in a jam-jar on my windowsill.
How big would my earwax model have
to get before it broke the world
record?

Yours faithfully,
Danny Baker
(Aged nearly ten)

WARNING! GROSSEST RECORDS YET!

Join Danny as he attempts to smash a
load of wacky records, including:

DEADLIEST ROLLERCOASTER RIDE!
FILTHIEST FURBALLS!
MOST BONKERS BIRTHDAY!

OUT NOW!

DANNY BAKER RECORD BREAKER

THE WORLD'S
WINDIEST BABY

STEVE HARTLEY

TO THE MANAGER
The Great Big Book
of World Records
London

Dear Sir,
Great news! I think my
brother Joey's going to be a
record breaker just like me!
His trouser-tearing trumps, belly-
busting belches and rip-roaring
raspberries are Mega-Ace! He
won the Fart-propelled Pushchair
competition at playgroup and his burps
can knock cats out of trees!
I'm so proud – is he the World's
Windiest Baby?
          Yours faithfully,
          Danny Baker
          (Aged ten and a half)

WARNING!
MORE
DANNY BAKER
BOOKS
AVAILABLE!

Join Danny as he attempts to smash a
load of madcap records, including:

TALLEST PIZZA TOWER!
BIGGEST UNDERPANT-HAT!
MOST INFECTIOUS YAWN!
COMING SOON!

Website Discount Offer

Get 3 for 2 on any of the Danny Baker series at www.panmacmillan.com

£1 postage and packaging costs to UK addresses, £2 for overseas

To buy the books with this special discount:

1. visit our website, www.panmacmillan.com
2. search by author or book title
3. add to your shopping basket

Closing date is 30 September 2011.

Full terms and conditions can be found at www.panmacmillan.com

Registration is required to purchase books from the website.

The offer is subject to availability of stock and applies to paperback editions only.